T0380918

GAROO

By Jeffrey Otersen

To order additional copies of this book, contact:
Xlibris
844-714-8691
www.Xlibris.com
Orders@Xlibris.com

ISBN: Softcover   979-8-3694-1798-0
         EBook   979-8-3694-1797-3

Print information available on the last page

Rev. date: 03/18/2024

"I dedicate this book to my daughter Braisley. She was born on June 21st, World Giraffe day. Giraffes are her favorite animal. Braisley is now thirteen. When she was younger I started writing the story of Garoo. Braisley named her 1st stuffed animal giraffe Garoo. I give special Thanks to my son Braiden for his idea of the character Boselli the W.W. II pigeon. I also give Thanks to my son Brennen for his wisdom and introducing me to Liz Cox, the Illustrator of Garoo. Thanks Liz for your dedication and great art work. Thanks to my wife Theresa for her support. I hope everyone who reads Garoo will enjoy and adore this story as much as Braisley."

"**R**un-Run-Run!" shouts a Baboon up high in the treetop, watching a baby Giraffe trying to outrun a Cheetah through his binoculars. "I'm gonna catch you!" utters the Cheetah, sounding grim.

The Giraffe kicks up dirt trying to get away. Suddenly, the Cheetah leaps high in the air and pounces on the little Giraffe, rolling him round and round on the ground. The Cheetah lands on top of the Giraffe, now face to face.

The Cheetah exposes his fangs. "Garoo, I could kill you in a second and you would be dead. It's a good thing I'm a vegetarian!" Garoo bursts with laughter. The Cheetah shakes his head. "Garoo, you've got to take this more seriously." Garoo cries out. "Magnus, it's your tail tick-tick-tickling my ribs."

Magnus unpins Garoo. The little Giraffe stands up looking wobbly while catching his breath. Garoo gasps. "That was a good race! I'll be faster next time."

The Baboon climbs down from the tree and looks at his stopwatch. "You dog gone better be!" replies Papio, looking concerned. Garoo, looking worn out, gives Papio a wince. "So, how slow was I? Papio scratches his head. "Well, ah… Hmmm. Garoo, there's no easy way to say this. You ran forty-five m.p.h.; a full-grown Cheetah can run up to seventy-five m.p.h. You gotta run faster. It's a dog-eat-dog world in this Jungle." Garoo gulps. Okay-okay. I'll work harder, I promise. I won't give up. Someday I'm going to run in the greatest race - The Horseshoe Cup!"

Magnus shakes his head. "It's nice to have dreams, but look around boy, we're in a Jungle! I'm just trying to help you survive by running faster, so the other Cheetahs don't eat you!"

Papio speaks up. "Let the boy have his dreams. He's got a gift from the Gods above. Someday he will be the fastest animal in the Jungle!" Garoo smiles. "Thanks, you two! Without the both of you, I would've been a meal for another animal a long time ago. Magnus, you saved me from a pack of Cheetahs that killed my Mom and Dad. And you also turned away from your pack to protect me, day and night. Papio, you help me with your wisdom. Collecting the right foods to make me stronger and keep me healthy."

A hummingbird chirps loudly from a treetop. Garoo looks up. "And, of course, you too, Colekio. Thanks for always watching my every step from high above and bringing me good luck!"

Magnus tells Garoo. "It's time to rest your muscles. You worked hard today. Tomorrow we will start training early." Garoo nods. "Okay, goodnight, Magnus, Papio, and Colekio." Then Garoo lays down in a bed of grass.

The next morning, the sun rises over the Jungle. Magnus wakes the crew. "It's time to rise and shine!" Garoo stands up while he yawns. "It's so early, can't we start a little later?"

Magnus shakes his head. "No pain - no gain! Please, Garoo, stretch your legs and line up on the starting line. I have a little surprise when you're ready."

Garoo giggles. "I love surprises!" Magnus yells. "Come on out!" A pack of Rhinos step out from the Jungle and line up behind Garoo. "Surprise!" Magnus shouts and then blows his whistle.

Garoo takes off running fast, leaving the herd of Rhinos in the dust. After a few laps, Garoo begins to slow down as his legs begin to tire. The Rhinos gain on him, getting closer and closer.

Garoo begins to worry as the Rhinos are hot on his hooves. The herd of Rhinos begin to chant. "Run, baby, run! Run, baby, run!" Just as the Rhinos are about to poke Garoo in the behind, Magnus blows his whistle, and the Rhinos stop in their tracks. Garoo lets out a huge sigh of relief as he collapses. "Whoooeh! That was too close for comfort."

Papio yaks loudly. "You ran 10 m.p.h. faster!" Garoo shouts, "Woo-hoo!"

After months of training with the Rhinos, Garoo's legs have grown and are now ten times stronger. Garoo outruns the Rhinos, leaving them way behind with no chance of catching him. Magnus tells Garoo. "It's time for the final test. I will chase you, and if I catch you, it's back to training."

Papio blows the whistle. Garoo takes off running. Magnus runs behind Garoo, trying to catch up, but Garoo is too fast.

Suddenly, Magnus sees a Man with a gun aiming at Garoo. "Stop, Garoo! Stop! There's danger up ahead!" Garoo snickers. "I'm not falling for any tricks today."

Garoo looks back and sticks out his tongue as he runs straight towards the shooter. Garoo sees the herd of Rhinos running rapidly into the Jungle. "Why is everyone running away when I'm winning the race?" he thinks to himself.

The Rhinos cry out. "They have come to steal our precious horns!" Garoo looks puzzled. "Who? What!" Garoo turns around to see a man with a gun. "Ohhh! NOOOO! I understand now." Garoo stops but he skids across the ground.

The Man fires his gun, and a speeding tranquilizer dart strikes Garoo in the behind. "Ouch!" yells Garoo and then he stumbles while becoming sleepy and tumbles over on his side.

The Man throws a net over Garoo and hoists him up on the back of a truck.

Magnus runs towards the truck as fast as he can, showing his fangs, hoping to scare him off.

The man runs to his truck and speeds away. Magnus shouts, "Garoo! Garoo!", Tears stream down his face as the truck disappears in a cloud of dust.

The next day, Garoo wakes up. He looks around, trying to focus. "Whoa! Everything is so blurry." A large Gorilla is looking over Garoo. "You'll be just fine in a few hours. The drug is wearing off." Garoo lifts his head while blinking. "Papio, is that you?" The Gorilla looks puzzled. "I'm not your Pappy! Have you lost your mind?" Garoo stands up, feeling woozy. He sees steel bars. "I don't think I broke any laws, so why am I in Jail?"

The Gorilla looks grim. "Sorry, kid! This place is now your new home. It's called a zoo." Garoo cries out. "Whaat!? This can't be happening. I need to go back to the Jungle in Africa." The Gorilla chuckles. "Oh, this place is kind of like a Jungle, but it's in Cincinnati." Garoo's eyes widen as he see's a airplane overhead pulling a banner that reads, "The Great Horseshoe Cup race is next Sunday". "This must be the plan from the Gods above. I must get out of here and get to the famous race, the Horseshoe Cup. It's next weekend."

The Gorilla laughs. "One problem - you're not a horse!" Garoo smirks. "I know, but it's my dream to race against the fastest horses in the world. I've been training really hard my whole life, for this race in Kentucky."

The Gorilla shakes his head. "It doesn't matter how hard you've trained; you're not getting out of here." The Gorilla tries to pull apart the steel bars with all his might. "Solid steel! No one is getting out of here." Garoo frantically yells. "Oh no! What am I gonna do? I gotta get out of here and get back to my friends in Africa!"

A Flamingo walk's over to the cage. "Hi, I'm a greeter, my name is Flamincia. Sorry for eavesdropping. I overheard your conversation. I can help you get to your race on time." Garoo questions Flamincia. "How are you gonna do that? I'm sorry, but you're not as strong as Beastie-boy here, so how are you gonna pry these bars apart?" Flamincia rolls her eyes. "I'm not mighty and strong, but I have connections." Flamincia goes on to explain. "I can't fly so they let me roam the zoo. I know everyone here. The visitors love to feed us. Anyways, I have friends who can help you."

Garoo smiles. "Oh, okay! It's worth a shot. Speaking of shots, I gotta lay back down, I still feel sleepy."

Flamincia asks Garoo. "Who are your friends in Africa?" Garoo answers in a tired voice. "There's Papio, my trainer. He's a Baboon that keeps watch up high in the trees. And Magnus, a Cheetah who looks after me, keeping me safe. Also, my good luck charm, Colekio, a hummingbird sent from the Heavens above."

Flamincia tells Garoo. "I'll be back later to tell you the plan."

Flamincia walks over to the shelter house where all the pigeons hang out.

"Psss! Hey, Boselli, I got a mission for you. It's Top Secret." A pigeon wearing a brown bomber jacket and a green army helmet flies down from the corner rafter where he hides. "Did you say 'Top Secret'?" Flamincia looks around, making sure that no one can hear. "Yes, Boselli, Top Secret. It's called Operation Horseshoe Cup." Boselli stands tall on a fence rail. "Ah, yes, finally I get to serve again. I haven't flown a mission since World War II, but I'm ready to fly again."

Flamincia thinks for a moment. "Boselli, I need you to fly across the Ocean to Africa and deliver a message to a Baboon named Papio. He's a trainer for a Giraffe named Garoo, who is going to be in a spectacular horse race next weekend."

"Did you say Giraffe?"

Flamincia picks up an ice cream wrapper and a twig off the ground. She dips the twig into the melted chocolate ice cream that was spilled on the ground by a guest.

Flamincia writes a message. "Garoo is in The Horseshoe Cup race in Kentucky. Next Sunday - Be There." She rolls it and attaches it to Boselli's ankle with a bread-tie, that was on top of the trash can. She tells Boselli. "Yes, I did say 'Giraffe'. I know, but it's his dream! We only have a week to make this happen." Flamincia salutes Boselli. "This must be a successful flight!"

Boselli salutes Flamincia as he prepares for takeoff. He zips his jacket, pulls down his goggles, and tightens his chin strap on his helmet. Then he starts flapping his wings radically and flies out of the zoo.

After two days of flight, Boselli lands in Africa. Boselli spots a group of Chimpanzees eating bananas in a treetop and playing the bongo. "Excuse me."

An old Chimpanzee climbs down from the tree. He stays in the tree, being cautious.

"Hey, ole chap, do you know a lad named Papio?" asks Boselli.

The old, long-bearded Chimp stares at Boselli. "I do." The old Chimp pauses for a moment. "What do you want with Papio?"

Boselli walks towards the tree. "That's close enough. Any closer and we will attack!" warns the Chimp. All the Chimpanzees put their war paint on their faces. Boselli, still out of breath from his long flight says, "I promise, I come in peace. It's kind of a long, crazy story, but I'll give you the gist of it!"

"I'm all ears," replies the Chimp.

"I'm looking for a trainer named Papio. I have a Top-Secret Message to deliver to him - and only him, Sir.", explains Boselli.

The old Chimp glares deviously. "First, the Giraffe gets kidnapped, and now you ask me the whereabouts of Papio. I can't tell you unless you give me more to go on. I won't jeopardize my brother's freedom."

Boselli starts to stutter. "I-I-I don't know - I can't remember. I'm old and forgetful. The only thing I can remember is Flamincia telling me this is a Top-Secret Mission called Operation Horseshoe Cup." Then Boselli looks down and he sees the note and takes it off and reads it. Garoo is in the Horseshoe cup race in Kentucky. Next Sunday - Be There." Garoo is a Giraffe who is going to race against Thoroughbreds - the fastest horses on earth" explains Boseli. Then Boselli bursts with laughter and wipes tears from his eyes. "Sorry, I don't think he stands a chance."

The old Chimp shouts. "Papio! Papio! Get over here I found Garoo!" Papio and Magnus hear the Chimp. They come running as fast as they can, with Colekio flying high above them.

"Where? Where is he?" They ask. Boselli answers. "He's in the Cincinnati Zoo. But he's on his way to the greatest horse race in Kentucky - The Horseshoe Cup!" Magnus's jaw drops. "What!" Boselli repeats himself. "He's in the Cincinnati Zoo, but he's on his way…" "Yes, I know, the greatest horse race in Kentucky, the Horseshoe Cup," interrupts Magnus. Then he says, "I've only heard this a million times."

Boselli looks at his stopwatch. "It's now fourteen hundred hours. We have a tight schedule. We have only five days and forty-six minutes till the race begins."

Papio shakes his head. "No, no. That's not enough time to travel. We're thousands of miles away and there's an ocean between us."

"That's a big problem. I can't swim," replies Magnus, looking heartbroken. "I will miss Garoo's dream day."

Boselli looks around at the Animals, all of them looking grim. "No worries. I will get you there. No one is missing this race!"

"What? Are we all gonna fly there?" exclaims Papio. "Yes! Yes, Papio, you are a genius! Wings are faster than legs." exclaims Boselli.

Papio laughs. "I was kidding. We don't have wings." Then Papio whispers to Magnus. "This guy is nuts!"

Boselli takes a moment while sipping from his canteen. "I'll be back." He starts flapping his wings and flies up. He shouts to the Animals. "I'm going to get wings." Magnus lets out a sigh. "Oh, boy. You're right, Papio, he's got a screw loose."

Papio, Magnus, and Colekio go back to tell the Rhinos the good news, that Garoo is alive.

A few days pass by. Papio tells Rhea and Magnus, "I sure hope our boy wins that race!"

"I sure hope he's ready for the challenge. He only gets one shot to show the World his gift." exclaims Rhea. "I'd do anything to see it." replies Magnus.

Suddenly, all the Animals hear a horrendous noise coming from the sky. "Look, it's Boselli! The war vet. He's back with a helicopter!" excitedly shouts Papio.

Boselli lands the helicopter in a meadow as it teeters back and forth, looking a little wobbly. "I'm a little rusty, but you can count on me. I'm an old pro! I used to fly these around back at the base a long time ago."

Papio, amazed by the helicopter, asks Boselli, "Where in the world did you get a helicopter?!"

Boselli chuckles, "I called in favor at the air base. Those ole boys owed me a favor."

Papio replies "That must've been some favor!".

Boselli grins, "I saved their butts back in WWII!"

Magnus takes a deep breath. "I'm also scared of heights. I can't do it!" Papio climbs aboard and Colekio flies in. "Come on, Magnus. You said you would do anything to see it!" Colekio chirps loudly.

"Thanks, Colekio, for reminding me." Papio looks at Magnus. "Remember telling Garoo, 'No Pain - No Gain'." Magnus gulps. "I-I-I… Yes. I said that!" Papio blows his whistle.

The pack of Rhinos start running towards Magnus. "Papio, make 'em stop! They're gonna prod me to death!" Papio shouts, "You must practice what you preach!" Magnus sees the Rhinos charging towards him. He's got nowhere to run to. The Rhinos close in. Magnus sprints while closing his eyes and leaps onto the helicopter, just in time, before he gets poked by their sharp horns.

One of the Rhinos jumps on the helicopter right behind Magnus. "Rhea, you can't poke me now," teases Magnus as he sticks his tongue out.

Rhea announces. "I'm not missing this race, not with all the hard work I put in to get Garoo to run faster." Magnus nods. "I agree. It's a team effort." The helicopter takes flight into the sky. They fly all day and night.

17

Meanwhile, back at the Cincinnati Zoo, Flamincia waits until it's dark and everyone has gone. She picks the lock with a popsicle stick and lets Garoo out. The Gorilla tells Garoo, "Good luck, kid!" Flamincia looks at the Gorilla. "Come on, Bongo. It's the chance of a lifetime!"

Bongo gets up and puts on his cap while strutting out of the cage. "I wish I could've pried the bars apart. I really wanted to!" "We know, we know you're strong, but sometimes we all need a little help from our friends," exclaims Flamincia. The three of them begin their journey to Kentucky.

A few days later, Boselli arrives at the horse track and hovers over it, just before the race begins. All the horses line up at the starting gate. Magnus looks around. "I don't see Garoo anywhere!" He exclaims, looking anxious. Colekio chirps and points. "Yes, yes! Thanks, Colekio. I see him!" says Papio as he spots Garoo at the back door of the racetrack.

"No worries, Magnus. Garoo is here!" Informs Papio. Then a loud sound erupts. "BANG!" The blast of a starting gun sets the horses off on the race. The helicopter starts to spin around and around. Boselli has flashbacks of the war he was once in a long time ago and becomes delusional.

Papio, worriedly exclaims, "Oh no the race has started without Garoo. He's gonna have some catching up to do." Magnus replies, "He's forged in fire, he's got this."

Meanwhile, the sound of the bang sends Boselli into a whirlwind. "We're under fire!" he shouts as he sees the flying V formation of Geese heading towards them. Boselli swerves radically left and back to right.

Magnus and Papio hold on tight, fearing for their lives. Boselli maneuvers the Huey medical helicopter up and down in a jerking motion. "Take cover! The enemy is attacking!" shouts Boselli. Magnus extracts his claws to grip the floor, but Papio falls out the side door of the helicopter. He swiftly grabs onto the land rail.

Papio holds on with one hand and watches through his binoculars with the other hand. "Oh no! Garoo can't get in the back door. It's locked!" Magnus looks out. "Who's that big hairy dude and the pink chick wearing a sombrero?" Papio scratches his head. "It appears I've been replaced."

Rhea speaks up. "Nonsense! Papio, you know that would never happen."

Suddenly, they all see the Gorilla rip the chains apart and Garoo enters the stall area. "Thanks, Bongo!" says Garoo as he looks around and sees saddles with numbers on the side.

Flamincia asks Garoo. "What number do you want?" Garoo points to the saddle with the number thirteen. Flamincia sighs. "That's not a lucky number!" Garoo nods. "I don't need luck. I'm going to prove that by wearing the Superstitious Thirteen!"

Flamincia laughs. "You got guts, kid!" Then she saddles Garoo and hops on with her wings wrapped tightly around his neck.

The pack of horses' round turn 3. Garoo rushes into the race galloping as fast as he can behind the pack of horses. "I'm behind the eight ball. I don't know if I can catch up." Flamincia hunkers down. "That's okay, kid. I believe in you. Now show me what you've got!"

Garoo starts to gain on the pack of horses. Now a half of a lap down, he sees the yellow flag waving as he passes the Grandstand. "We only have one more lap!" announces Flamincia then Garoo kicks into high gear.

Magnus and Papio hold on for dear life as the helicopter spins out of control.

"Mayday-Mayday, we've been hit!" shouts Boselli as the squad of Geese pass over, dropping poo-poo on the helicopter. Rhea drops down with her horn sticking out of the helicopter. "Grab my horn Papio before you get hit!"

Papio swings up and latches onto Rhea's horn. She pulls him back into the helicopter just as they are bombarded by poo-poo.

"Um! Somebody should check what that old bird has been sipping on in that canteen. That was a bunch of Geese! Not airplanes!" exclaims Rhea. "Whoo, that was a close one!" cries out Papio while wiping his brow.

"Take it easy Bro! We're all okay. It's not gunfire or war planes," informs Rhea.

"No, it's Bo. That's my nickname. And you're right. I'm sweating bullets over nothing. I'm sorry!" exclaims Bozelli. Colekio chirps loudly. They all look down to see Garoo rounding the last corner.

"I'm on the home stretch!" yells Garoo as he goes into third place.

"I don't know if I can catch the other two horses, I'm running out of gas!" yells Garoo. "It's time to use your head!" shouts Flamincia as dirt kicks up around the horses. Garoo looks puzzled.

"Oh yeah, my head!" he answers, Garoo lowers his head and his long neck stretches out past the other two horses as they cross the finish line.

"He won! He Won! Our boy won!" Papio and Magnus give each other a big hug while Colekio begins to sing.

Back on the field, Flamincia tells Garoo. "I knew you could do it!"

Garoo slows down and realizes that Colekio is here as he hears a sweet humming melody coming from above.

The helicopter lands in the middle of the field. Magnus, Papio, and Rhea burst out of the helicopter and run onto the track.

Garoo can't believe his eyes as he sees his family. "You made it! I thought you all missed it!" Papio smiles along with Magnus."We wouldn't miss it for all the tea in China!" exclaims Papio while Colekio hums a victory tune.

Garoo looks up. "I knew my good luck charm wasn't far away!" Garoo takes a bow and yells out, "Wah-lah!" as fireworks light up the sky.

25

THE END

About the Author

I was born and raised in Toledo, Ohio. I currently live in Sylvania, Ohio. I have been working in the Trucking industry for 37 years. Writing books is my passion.

Printed in the United States
by Baker & Taylor Publisher Services